P9-CEL-166

CHILDREN'S THRIFT CLASSICS

The Ugly Duckling and Other Fairy Tales

HANS CHRISTIAN ANDERSEN

Illustrated by Harriet Golden

DOVER PUBLICATIONS, INC.
New York

DOVER CHILDREN'S THRIFT CLASSICS
EDITOR: PHILIP SMITH

Copyright © 1992 by Dover Publications, Inc.
All rights reserved under Pan American and International Copyright Conventions.

Published in Canada by General Publishing Company, Ltd., 30 Lesmill Road, Don Mills, Toronto, Ontario.

Published in the United Kingdom by Constable and Company, Ltd., 3 The Lanchesters, 162–164 Fulham Palace Road, London W6 9ER.

This Dover edition, first published in 1992, is a new selection of fairy tales by Hans Christian Andersen. Seven of the tales are taken from *Andersen's Fairy Tales*, edited by Margherita O. Osbourne, published by The Hampton Publishing Company, New York, 1930. The eighth, "The Little Match Girl," is from a standard edition. The illustrations and an introductory note have been specially prepared for this edition.

Manufactured in the United States of America
Dover Publications, Inc., 31 East 2nd Street, Mineola, N.Y. 11501

Library of Congress Cataloging-in-Publication Data

Andersen, H. C. (Hans Christian), 1805–1875.
    The ugly duckling and other fairy tales / Hans Christian Andersen ; illustrated by Harriet Golden.
        p.   cm. — (Dover children's thrift classics)
    Contents: The ugly duckling — The emperor's new clothes — The princess on the pea — The red shoes — The steadfast tin soldier — Thumbelina — The little match girl — The nightingale.
    ISBN 0-486-27081-5 (pbk.)
    1. Fairy tales—Denmark. 2. Children's stories, Danish—Translations into English. 3. Children's stories, English—Translations from Danish. [1. Fairy tales.] I. Golden, Harriet, ill. II. Title. III. Series.
PZ8.A542Ug   1992b
[Fic]—dc20   91–47565
                                                                                    CIP
                                                                                    AC

Note

Although his name has become virtually synonymous with children's literature, the Danish writer Hans Christian Andersen (1805–1875) tried his hand unsuccessfully at a number of careers and literary forms before publishing his first volume of *Eventyr, fortalte for Børn* ("Tales Told for Children") in 1835. These tales, published a handful at a time in small annual collections, soon attracted a devoted audience of all ages and were translated into many languages, bringing their author international acclaim.

Written in a deliberately rough style suggestive of verbal storytelling, Andersen's fairy tales can be enjoyed both as children's narratives and as wry autobiographical satires of the adult world. Blending folk tales with plots of his own invention, Andersen developed a distinctive literary type of original tale for children, a form that is still frequently imitated.

Contents

List of Illustrations

The Ugly Duckling

IN A SUNNY SPOT in the country stood an old mansion surrounded by a deep moat. Great dock leaves grew from the walls of the house right down to the water's edge; some of them were so tall that a small child could stand upright under them. In amongst the leaves it was as secluded as in the depths of a forest; and there a duck was sitting on her nest. Her little ducklings were just about to be hatched, but she was nearly tired of sitting; it had lasted such a long time. Moreover, she had very few visitors, as the other ducks liked swimming about in the moat better than waddling up to sit under the dock leaves and gossip with her.

At last one egg after another began to crack. "Cheep, cheep!" they said. All the chicks had come to life, and were poking out their heads.

"Quack! quack!" said the duck; they all

1

quacked their hardest, and looked about them on all sides among the green leaves; their mother allowed them to look as much as they liked, for green is good for the eyes.

"How big the world is, to be sure!" said all the young ones; for they certainly had ever so much more room to move about than when they were inside in the egg shell.

"Do you imagine this is the whole world?" said the mother. "It stretches a long way on the other side of the garden, right into the parson's field; but I have never been as far as that! I suppose you are all here now?" and she got up. "No! I declare I have not got you all yet! The biggest egg is still there; how long is it going to last?" and she settled herself on the nest again.

"Well, how are you getting on?" said an old duck who had come to pay her a visit.

"This one egg is taking such a long time," answered the sitting duck, "the shell will not crack; but now you must look at the others; they are the finest ducklings I have ever seen! they are all exactly like their father, the rascal! he never comes to see me."

"Let me look at the egg that won't crack," said the old duck. "You may be sure that it is a turkey's egg! I have been cheated like that once, and I had no end of trouble and worry with the creatures, for I may tell you that they are afraid of the water. I could not get them into it; I quacked and snapped at them, but it was no good. Let me see the egg! Yes, it is a turkey's egg! You just let it alone and teach the other children to swim."

"I will sit on it a little longer; I have sat so long already, that I may as well go on till the Midsummer Fair comes round."

"Please yourself," said the old duck, and she went away.

At last the big egg cracked. "Cheep, cheep!" said the young one and tumbled out; how big and ugly he was! The duck looked at him.

"That is a monstrous big duckling," she said; "none of the others looked like that; can he be a turkey chick? Well, we shall soon find that out; into the water he shall go, if I have to kick him in myself."

Next day was gloriously fine, and the sun shone on all the green dock leaves. The mother duck with her whole family went down to the moat.

Splash, into the water she sprang. "Quack, quack!" she said, and one duckling plumped in after the other. The water dashed over their heads, but they came up again and floated

"Cheep, cheep!" said the young one and
tumbled out.

beautifully; their legs went of themselves, and they were all there; even the big ugly gray one swam about with them.

"No, that is no turkey," she said. "How beautifully he uses his legs and how erect he holds himself: he is my own chick! after all, he is not so bad when you come to look at him properly. Quack, quack! Now come with me and I will take you into the world, and introduce you to the duckyard; but keep close to me all the time, so that no one may tread upon you, and beware of the cat!"

They went into the duckyard. There was a fearful uproar going on, for two broods were fighting for the head of an eel, and in the end the cat captured it.

"That's how things go in this world," said the mother duck, and she licked her bill, for she wanted the eel's head herself.

"Use your legs," said she; "mind you quack properly, and bend your necks to the old duck over there! She is the grandest of them all; she has Spanish blood in her veins and that accounts for her size, and, do you see? she has a red rag round her leg; that is a wonderfully fine thing, and the most extraordinary mark of distinction any duck can have. It shows clearly that she is not to be parted with, and that she is worthy of recognition both by beasts and men! Quack now! don't turn your toes in; a well brought up duckling keeps his legs wide apart just like father and mother; that's it, now bend your necks, and say quack!"

They did as they were bid, but the other ducks round about looked at them and said, quite loud: "Just look there! now we are to have that tribe! just as if there were not enough of us already, and, oh, dear! how ugly that duckling is; we won't stand him!" and a duck flew at him at once and bit him in the neck.

"Let him be," said the mother; "he is doing no harm."

"Very likely not, but he is so ungainly and queer," said the biter; "he must be whacked."

"They are handsome children mother has," said the old duck with the rag round her leg; "all good looking except this one. He is not a good specimen; it's a pity you can't make him over again."

"That can't be done, your grace," said the mother duck; "he is not handsome, but he is a thorough good creature, and he swims as beautifully as any of the others; nay, I think I might venture even to add that I think he will improve as he goes on, or perhaps in time he may grow smaller! He was too long in the egg, and so he has not come out with a very good figure." She patted his neck and stroked him down. "Besides he is a drake," said she; "so it does not matter so much. I believe he will be very strong, and I don't doubt but he will make his way in the world."

"The other ducklings are very pretty," said the old duck. "Now make yourselves quite at home, and if you find the head of an eel you may bring it to me!"

After that they felt quite at home. But the poor duckling which had been the last to come out of the shell, and who was so ugly, was bitten, pushed about, and made fun of both by the ducks and the hens. "He is too big," they all said; and the turkey-cock, who was born with his spurs on, and therefore thought himself quite an emperor, puffed himself up like a vessel in full sail, made for him, and gobbled and gobbled till he became quite red in the face. The poor duckling was at his wit's end, and did not know which way to turn; he was in despair because he was so ugly, and the butt of the whole duckyard.

So the first day passed, and afterwards matters grew worse and worse. The poor duckling was chased and hustled by all of them; even his brothers and sisters abused him; and they were always saying, "If only the cat

would get hold of you, you hideous object!"
Even his mother said, "I wish to goodness you
were miles away." The ducks bit him, the
hens pecked him, and the girl who fed them
kicked him aside.

At last he ran off and flew right over the
hedge, where the little birds flew up into the
air in a fright.

"That is because I am so ugly," thought the
poor duckling, shutting his eyes, but he ran on
all the same until he came to a great marsh
where the wild ducks lived; he was so tired
and miserable that he stayed there the whole
night.

In the morning the wild ducks flew up to
inspect their new comrade.

"What sort of a creature are you?" they
inquired, as the duckling turned from side to
side and greeted them as well as he could.
"You are frightfully ugly," said the wild ducks,
"but that does not matter to us, so long as you
do not marry into our family!" Poor fellow! he
had not thought of marriage; all he wanted
was permission to lie among the rushes, and
to drink a little of the marsh water.

He stayed there two whole days, then two
wild geese came, or rather two wild ganders;
they were not long out of the shell, and therefore rather pert.

"I say, comrade," they said, "you are so ugly that we have taken quite a fancy to you; will you join us and be a bird of passage? There is another marsh close by, and there are some charming wild geese there; all sweet young ladies, who can say quack! You are ugly enough to make your fortune among them." Just at that moment, bang! bang! was heard up above, and both the wild geese fell dead among the reeds, and the water turned blood red. Bang! bang! went the guns, and whole flocks of wild geese flew up from the rushes and the shot peppered among them again.

There was a grand shooting party, and the sportsmen lay hidden round the marsh; some even sat on the branches of the trees which overhung the water; the blue smoke rose like clouds among the dark trees and swept over the pool.

The water-dogs wandered about in the swamp, splash! splash! The rushes and reeds bent beneath their tread on all sides. It was terribly alarming to the poor duckling. He twisted his head round to get it under his wing, and just at that moment a frightful, big dog appeared close beside him; his tongue hung right out of his mouth and his eyes glared wickedly. He opened his great chasm of a mouth close to the duckling, showed his sharp teeth—and—splash—went on without touching him.

"Oh, thank Heaven!" sighed the duckling, "I am so ugly that even the dog won't bite me!"

Then he lay quite still while the shot whistled among the bushes, and bang after bang rent the air. It only became quiet late in the day, but even then the poor duckling did not dare to get up; he waited several hours more before he looked about, and then he hurried away from the marsh as fast as he could. He ran across fields and meadows, and there was such a wind that he had hard work to make his way.

Towards night he reached a poor little cottage; it was such a miserable hovel that it could not make up its mind which way to fall even, and so it remained standing. The wind whistled so fiercely round the duckling that he had to sit on his tail to resist it, and it blew harder and harder; then he saw that the door had fallen off one hinge and hung so crookedly that he could creep into the house through the crack, and by this means he made his way into the room. An old woman lived there with her cat and her hen. The cat, which she called "Sonnie," could arch his back, purr, and give off electric sparks, that is to say if you stroked his fur the wrong way. The hen had quite tiny short legs, and so she was called "Chuckie-low-legs." She laid good eggs, and the old woman was as fond of her as if she had been her own child.

In the morning the strange duckling was immediately discovered and the cat began to purr, and the hen to cluck.

"What on earth is that!" said the old woman, looking round, but her sight was not good, and she thought the duckling was a fat duck which had escaped. "This is a capital find," said she; "now I shall have duck's eggs if only it is not a drake! we must find out about that!"

So she took the duckling on trial for three weeks, but no eggs made their appearance. The cat was the master of the house and the hen the mistress, and they always spoke of "we and the world," for they thought that they represented the half of the world, and that quite the better half.

The duckling thought there might be two opinions on the subject, but the hen would not hear of it.

"Can you lay eggs?" she asked.

"No!"

"Will you have the goodness to hold your tongue then!"

And the cat said, "Can you arch your back, purr, or give off sparks?"

"No."

"Then you had better keep your opinions to yourself when people of sense are speaking!"

The duckling sat in the corner nursing his ill-humor; then he began to think of the fresh air and the sunshine, an uncontrollable longing seized him to float on the water, and at last he could not help telling the hen about it.

"What on earth possesses you?" she asked; "you have nothing to do, that is why you get these freaks into your head. Lay some eggs or take to purring, and you will get over it."

"But it is so delicious to float on the water," said the duckling; "so delicious to feel it rushing over your head when you dive to the bottom."

"That would be a fine amusement," said the hen. "I think you have gone mad. Ask the cat about it; he is the wisest creature I know; ask him if he is fond of floating on the water or diving under it. I say nothing about myself. Ask our mistress, the old woman; there is no one in the world cleverer than she is. Do you suppose she has any desire to float on the water, or to duck underneath it?"

"You do not understand me," said the duckling.

"Well, if we don't understand you, who should? I suppose you don't consider yourself cleverer than the cat or the old woman, not to mention me. Don't make a fool of yourself, child, and thank your stars for all the good we have done you! Have you not lived in this warm room, and in such society that you might have learned something? But you are an idiot, and there is no pleasure in associating with you. You may believe me I mean you well, I tell you home truths, and there is no surer way than that of knowing who are one's friends. You just see about laying some eggs, or learn to purr, or to emit sparks."

"I think I will go out into the wide world," said the duckling.

"Oh, do so by all means," said the hen.

So away went the duckling; he floated on the water and ducked underneath it, but he was looked askance at by every living creature for his ugliness. Now the autumn came on; the leaves in the woods turned yellow and brown; the wind took hold of them, and they danced about. The sky looked very cold, and the clouds hung heavy with snow and hail. A raven stood on the fence and croaked caw! caw! from sheer cold; it made one shiver only to think of it; the poor duckling certainly was in a bad case.

One evening, the sun was just setting in wintry splendor, when a flock of beautiful large birds appeared out of the bushes; the duckling had never seen anything so beautiful. They were dazzlingly white with long waving necks; they were swans, and uttering a peculiar cry, they spread out their magnificent broad wings and flew away from the cold regions to warmer lands and open seas. They mounted so high, so very high! The ugly little duckling became strangely uneasy; he circled round and round in the water like a wheel, craning his neck up into the air after them. Then he uttered a shriek so piercing and so strange, that he quite frightened himself. Oh, he could not forget those beautiful birds, those happy birds, and as soon as they were out of sight he ducked right down to the bottom, and when he came up again he was quite beside himself. He did not know what the birds were, or whither they flew, but all the same he was more drawn towards them than he had ever been by any creatures before. He did not envy them in the least; how could it occur to him even to wish to be such a marvel of beauty? He would have been thankful if only the ducks would have tolerated him among them—the poor ugly creature!

The winter was so bitterly cold that the duckling was obliged to swim about in the water to keep it from freezing, but every night the hole in which he swam got smaller and smaller. Then it froze so hard that the surface ice cracked, and the duckling had to use his legs all the time, so that the ice should not close in round him; at last he was so weary that he could move no more, and he was frozen fast into the ice.

Early in the morning a peasant came along and saw him; he went out onto the ice and hammered a hole in it with his heavy wooden shoe, and carried the duckling home to his wife. There it soon revived. The children wanted to play with it, but the duckling thought they were going to abuse him, and rushed in his fright into the milk pan, and the milk spurted out all over the room. The woman shrieked and threw up her hands. The duckling flew into the butter cask, and down into the meal tub and out again. Just imagine what it looked like by this time! The woman screamed and tried to hit it with the tongs, and the children tumbled over one another in trying to catch it, and they screamed with laughter—by good luck the door stood open, and the duckling flew out among the bushes and the new fallen snow—and it lay there thoroughly exhausted.

But it would be too sad to mention all the privation and misery it had to go through during that hard winter. When the sun began to shine warmly again, the duckling was in the marsh, lying among the rushes; the larks were singing and the beautiful spring had come.

When all at once it raised its wings, they flapped with much greater strength than before, and bore him off vigorously. Before he knew where he was, he found himself in a large garden where the apple trees were in full blossom, and the air was scented with lilacs; the long branches overhung the indented shores of the lake! Oh! the spring freshness was so delicious!

Just in front of him he saw three beautiful white swans advancing towards him from a thicket; with rustling feathers they swam lightly over the water. The duckling recognized the majestic birds, and he was overcome by a strange melancholy.

"I will fly to them, the royal birds, and they will hack me to pieces, because I, who am so ugly, venture to approach them! But it won't matter; better be killed by them than be snapped at by the ducks, pecked by the hens, or spurned by the henwife, or suffer so much misery in the winter."

So he flew into the water and swam towards the stately swans; they saw him and darted towards him with ruffled feathers.

"Kill me, oh, kill me!" said the poor creature, and bowing his head towards the water he awaited his death. But what did he see reflected in the transparent water?

He saw below him his own image, but he was no longer a clumsy dark gray bird, ugly and ungainly; he was himself a swan! It does not matter in the least having been born in a duckyard, if only you come out of a swan's egg!

He felt quite glad of all the misery and tribulation he had gone through; he was the better able to appreciate his good fortune now, and all the beauty which greeted him. The big swans swam round and round him, and stroked him with their bills.

Some little children came into the garden with corn and pieces of bread, which they threw into the water; and the smallest one cried out, "There is a new one!" The other children shouted with joy, "Yes, a new one has come!" And they clapped their hands and danced about, running after their father and mother. They threw the bread into the water, and one and all said: "The new one is the prettiest! He is so young and handsome." And the old swans bent their heads and did homage before him.

He felt quite shy, and hid his head under his

wing; he did not know what to think; he was so happy, but not at all proud; a good heart never becomes proud. He thought of how he had been pursued and scorned, and now he heard them all say that he was the most beautiful of all beautiful birds. The lilacs bent their boughs right down into the water before him, and the bright sun was warm and cheering, and he rustled his feathers and raised his slender neck aloft, saying with exultation in his heart: "I never dreamed of so much happiness when I was the Ugly Duckling!"

The Emperor's New Clothes

MANY YEARS AGO there was an emperor who was so very fond of new clothes that he spent all his money on them. He cared nothing about his soldiers nor about the theater, nor for driving in the woods except for the sake of showing off his new clothes. He had a costume for every hour in the day, and instead of saying as one does about any other king or emperor, "He is in his council chamber," they always said, "The emperor is in his dressing-room."

Life was very gay in the great town where he lived; hosts of strangers came to visit it every day. Among the visitors one day came two swindlers. They gave themselves out as weavers, and said that they knew how to weave the most beautiful stuffs imaginable. Not only were the colors and patterns unusually fine, but the clothes that were made of the cloth had the peculiar quality of becoming

19

invisible to anyone who was not fit for the office he held, or who was impossibly dull.

"Those must be splendid clothes," thought the emperor. "By wearing them I should be able to discover which men in my kingdom are unfitted for their posts. I shall distinguish the wise men from the fools. Yes, I certainly must order some of that stuff to be woven for me."

He paid the two swindlers a lot of money in advance, so that they might begin their work at once.

They did put up two looms and pretended to weave, but they had nothing whatever upon their shuttles. At the outset they asked for a quantity of the finest silk and the purest gold thread, all of which they put into their own bags while they worked away at the empty looms far into the night.

"I should like to know how those weavers are getting on with the stuff," thought the emperor; but he felt a little queer when he reflected that anyone who was stupid or unfit for his post would not be able to see it. He certainly thought that he need have no fears for himself, but still he thought he would send somebody else first to see how it was getting on. Everybody in the town knew what wonderful power the cloth possessed, and everyone was anxious to see how stupid his neighbor was.

"I will send my faithful old minister to the weavers," thought the emperor. "He will be best able to see how the stuff looks, for he is a clever man and no one fulfills his duties better than he does!"

So the good old minister went into the room where the two swindlers sat working at the empty loom.

"Heaven preserve us!" thought the old minister, opening his eyes very wide. "Why I can't see a thing!" But he took care not to say so.

Both the swindlers begged him to be good enough to step a little nearer, and asked if he did not think it a good pattern and beautiful coloring. They pointed to the empty loom, and the poor old minister stared as hard as he could, but he could not see anything, for of course there was nothing to see.

"Good heavens!" thought he, "is it possible that I am a fool? I have never thought so, and nobody must know it. Am I not fit for my post? It will never do to say that I cannot see the cloths."

"Well, sir, you don't say anything about the stuff," said the one who was pretending to weave.

"Oh, it is beautiful! quite charming!" said

the minister looking through his spectacles; "this pattern and these colors! I will certainly tell the emperor that the stuff pleases me very much."

"We are delighted to hear you say so," said the swindlers, and then they named all the colors and described the peculiar pattern. The old minister paid great attention to what they said, so as to be able to repeat it when he got home to the emperor.

Then the swindlers went on to demand more money, more silk, and more gold, to be able to proceed with the weaving, and they put it all into their own pockets—not a single strand was ever put into the loom, but they went on as before weaving at the empty loom.

The emperor soon sent another faithful official to see how the stuff was getting on, and if it would soon be ready. The same thing happened to him as to the minister; he looked and looked, but as there was only the empty loom, he could see nothing at all.

"Is not this a beautiful piece of stuff?" said both the swindlers, showing and explaining the beautiful pattern and colors which were not there to be seen.

"I know I am no fool!" thought the man, "so it must be that I am unfit for my good post! It is very strange though! however one must not let it appear!" So he praised the stuff he did not see, and assured them of his delight in the beautiful colors and the originality of the design. "It is absolutely charming!" he said to the emperor. Everybody in the town was talking about this splendid stuff.

Now the emperor thought he would like to see it while it was still on the loom. So, accompanied by a number of selected courtiers, among whom were the two faithful officials who had already seen the imaginary stuff, he went to visit the crafty impostors, who were working away as hard as ever they could at the empty loom.

"It is magnificent!" said both the honest officials. "Only see, your Majesty, what a design! What colors!" And they pointed to the empty loom, for they thought no doubt the others could see the stuff.

"What!" thought the emperor; "I see nothing at all! This is terrible! Am I a fool? Am I not fit to be emperor? Why, nothing worse could happen to me!"

"Oh, it is beautiful!" said the emperor. "It has my highest approval!" and he nodded his satisfaction as he gazed at the empty loom. Nothing would make him say that he could not see anything.

The whole suite gazed and gazed, but saw

nothing more than all the others. However, they all exclaimed with his Majesty, "It is very beautiful!" and they advised him to wear a suit made of this wonderful cloth on the occasion of a great procession which was just about to take place.

"It is magnificent! gorgeous! excellent!" went from mouth to mouth. They were all equally delighted with it. The emperor gave each of the rogues an order of knighthood to be worn in their buttonholes and the title of "Gentlemen weavers."

The swindlers sat up the whole night, before the day on which the procession was to take place, burning sixteen candles; so that people might see how anxious they were to get the emperor's new clothes ready. They pretended to take the stuff off the loom. They cut it out in the air with a huge pair of scissors, and they stitched away with needles without any thread in them. At last they said: "Now the emperor's new clothes are ready!"

The emperor, with his grandest courtiers, went to them himself, and both swindlers raised one arm in the air, as if they were holding something, and said: "See, these are the trousers, this is the coat, here is the mantle!" and so on. "It is as light as a spider's web. One

"See, these are the trousers, this is the coat, here
is the mantle!"

might think one had nothing on, but that is the very beauty of it!"

"Yes!" said all the courtiers, but they could not see anything, for there was nothing to see.

"Will your Imperial Majesty be graciously pleased to take off your clothes," said the impostors, "so that we may put on the new ones, along here before the great mirror."

The emperor took off all his clothes, and the impostors pretended to give him one article of dress after the other, of the new ones which they had pretended to make. They pretended to fasten something round his waist and to tie on the train, and the emperor turned round and round in front of the mirror.

"How well his Majesty looks in the new clothes! How becoming they are!" cried all the people around him. "What a design, and what colors! They are most gorgeous robes!"

"The canopy is waiting outside which is to be carried over your Majesty in the procession," said the master of the ceremonies.

"Well, I am quite ready," said the emperor. "Don't the clothes fit well?" and then he turned round again in front of the mirror, so that he should seem to be looking at his grand things.

The chamberlains who were to carry the

train stooped and pretended to lift it from the ground with both hands, and they walked along with their hands in the air. They dared not let it appear that they could not see anything.

Then the emperor walked along in the procession under the gorgeous canopy, and everybody in the streets and at the windows exclaimed, "How beautiful the emperor's new clothes are! What a splendid train! And they fit to perfection!" Nobody would let it appear that he could see nothing, for then he would be proved unfit for his post, or else a fool.

None of the emperor's clothes had been so successful before.

"But he has got nothing on," said a little child.

"Oh, listen to the innocent," said its father. Then one person whispered to the other what the child had said. "He has nothing on! A child says he has nothing on!"

"But he has nothing on!" at last cried all the people.

The emperor writhed, for he knew it was true, but he thought "the procession must go on now," so he held himself stiffer than ever, and the chamberlains held up the invisible train.

The Princess on the Pea

THERE WAS ONCE a prince, and he
wanted to marry a princess, but she must
be a real princess. He traveled right round the
world to find one, but there was always something wrong. There were plenty of princesses,
but whether they were real princesses he
couldn't make sure for there was always
something not quite right about them. So at
last he had to come home again, and he was
very sad because he wanted a real princess so
badly.

One evening there was a terrible storm;
with thunder and lightning and the rain pour-
ing down in torrents; it was a fearful night.

In the middle of the storm somebody
knocked at the town gate, and the old king
himself went to open it.

It was a princess who stood outside, but
she was in a terrible state from the rain and
the storm. The water streamed out of her hair

and her clothes, it ran in at the top of her shoes and out at the heel, but she said that she was a real princess.

"Well we shall soon see if that is true," thought the old queen, but she did not say so. She went into the bedroom where the princess was to sleep and took all the bedclothes off, then she laid a pea on the bedstead and took twenty mattresses and piled them on the top of the pea, and then twenty feather beds on the top of the mattresses. In the morning they asked the princess how she had slept.

"Oh terribly badly!" said the princess. "I have hardly closed my eyes the whole night! Heaven knows what was in the bed. I seemed to be lying upon some hard thing, and my whole body is black and blue this morning. It is terrible!"

They at once saw that she must be a real princess since she had felt the pea through twenty mattresses and twenty feather beds. Nobody but a real princess could have such a delicate skin.

So the prince took her to be his wife, for now he was sure that he had found a real princess, and the pea was put into a Museum, where it may still be seen if no one has stolen it.

Now this is a true story.

The Red Shoes

THERE WAS ONCE a tiny, delicate little girl, who was so poor that she always had to go about barefoot in summer. In winter she only had a pair of heavy wooden shoes, which chafed her ankles terribly.

An old mother shoemaker, who lived in the middle of the village, made a pair of little shoes out of some strips of red cloth. They were very clumsy, but she made them out of pity for the little girl whose name was Karen.

These shoes were given to her, and she wore them for the first time on the day her mother was buried; they were certainly not mourning, but she had no others, and so she walked barelegged in them behind the poor pine coffin.

A big old carriage happened to drive by, and a big old lady was seated in it; she looked at the little girl, and felt very, very sorry for her, and said to the parson, "Give the little girl to

me and I will look after her and be kind to
her." Karen thought it was all because of the
red shoes, but the old lady said they were hideous, and had them burned. Karen was well
and neatly dressed. She had to learn reading
and sewing. People said she was pretty, but
her mirror said, "You are more than pretty,
you are lovely."

One day the queen passed through that part
of the country; she had her little daughter the
princess with her. Karen, with many other
people, crowded round the palace where they
were staying, to see them. The little princess
appeared at a window. She wore neither a
train nor a golden crown, but she was dressed
all in white with a beautiful pair of red
morocco shoes. They were not at all like
those the poor old mother shoemaker had
made for Karen. She had never seen anything
as beautiful as these red shoes.

The time came when Karen was old enough
to be confirmed; she had new clothes, and she
was to have a pair of new shoes. The rich
shoemaker in the town was to take the mea-
sure of her little foot; his shop was full of
glass cases of the loveliest shoes and boots.
They looked tempting, but the old lady could
not see very well, so it gave her no pleasure to
look at them. Among all the other shoes there

was one pair of red shoes like those worn by the princess. Oh, how pretty they were! The shoemaker told them that they had been made for an earl's daughter, but they had not fitted. "I suppose they are patent leather," said the old lady, "they are so shiny."

"Yes, indeed, they do shine," said Karen, and she tried them on. They fitted and were bought; but the old lady had not the least idea that they were red. She would never have allowed Karen to wear red shoes for her Confirmation.

Everybody looked at Karen's feet when she walked up the church to the chancel; even the old pictures, those portraits of old priests and their wives, with stiff collars and long black clothes, seemed to fix their eyes upon her shoes. She thought of nothing else when the minister laid his hand upon her head and spoke to her of holy baptism, the covenant of God, and told her that from henceforth she was to be a responsible Christian person. The solemn notes of the organ resounded, the children sang with their sweet voices, the old precentor sang, but Karen thought of nothing but her red shoes.

By the afternoon several persons had told the old lady that the shoes were red, and she told Karen that it was very naughty and most improper. For the future, whenever Karen went to the church she was to wear black shoes, even if they were old. Next Sunday there was Holy Communion. Karen looked at the black shoes and then at the red ones — then she looked again at the red, and at last put them on.

It was beautiful, sunny weather; Karen and the old lady went by the path through the corn-field, which was rather dusty. By the church door stood a lame old soldier. He carried a crutch and he had a curious long beard, it was more red than white, in fact it was almost quite red. He bent down to the ground and asked the old lady if he might dust her shoes. Karen put out her little foot, too. "What beautiful dancing shoes!" said the soldier. "Mind you stick fast when you dance," and as he spoke he struck the soles with his hand. The old lady gave the soldier a copper and went into the church with Karen. All the people in the church looked at Karen's red shoes, and all the portraits looked, too. When Karen knelt at the altar-rails and the chalice was put to her lips, she only thought of the red shoes; she seemed to see them floating before her eyes. She forgot to join in the hymn of praise, and she forgot to say the Lord's Prayer.

When everybody left the church, and the

old lady got into her carriage, Karen lifted her foot to get in after her, but the old soldier, who was still standing there, said, "See what pretty dancing shoes!"

Karen couldn't help it; she took a few dancing steps. But when she had begun, her feet kept on dancing. The shoes seemed to have a power over them. She danced right round the church and couldn't stop; the coachman had to run after her and take hold of her, and lift her into the carriage; but her feet continued to dance, so that she kicked the poor lady horribly. At last they got the shoes off, and her feet had a little rest.

When they got home the shoes were put away in a cupboard, but Karen could not help going to look at them.

The old lady became very ill; she had to be carefully nursed and tended, and no one was nearer than Karen to do this. But there was to be a grand ball in the town, and Karen was invited. She looked at the old lady, and she looked at the red shoes. She thought there was no harm in doing so and she even put on the red shoes; but then she went to the ball and began to dance!

The shoes would not let her do what she liked: when she wanted to go to the right, they danced to the left: when she wanted to dance

But when she had begun, her feet kept on dancing.

up the room, the shoes danced down the room. They danced down the stairs, through the streets and out of the town gate. Away she danced, and away she had to dance, right away into the dark forest. Something shone up above the trees, and she thought it was the moon. But it was the face of the old soldier with the red beard, and he nodded and said, "See what pretty dancing shoes!"

This frightened her terribly and she tried to throw off the red shoes, but they stuck fast. She tore off her stockings, but the shoes had grown fast to her feet, and off she danced, and off she had to dance over fields and meadows, in rain and sunshine, by day and by night, but at night it was fearful.

She danced into the open churchyard, and she tried to sit down on a pauper's grave where the bitter wormwood grew, but there was no rest nor repose for her. When she danced towards the open church door, she saw an angel standing there in long white robes; his wings reached from his shoulders to the ground, his face was grave and stern, and in his hand he held a broad and shining sword.

"Dance and dance," said he, "you shall dance in your red shoes till you are pale and cold. You shall dance from door to door, and wherever you find proud vain children, you must knock at the door so that they may see you and fear you."

"Mercy!" shrieked Karen, but she did not hear the angel's answer, for the shoes bore her through the gate into the fields over roadways and paths, ever and ever she was forced to dance.

One morning she danced past a door she knew well; she heard the sound of a hymn from within, and she knew that the old lady was dead, and it seemed to her that she was forsaken by all the world.

On and on she danced; the shoes bore her over briars and stubble till her feet were torn and bleeding. She danced over the heath till she came to a little lonely house. She knew the executioner lived here, and she tapped with her fingers on the window pane and said,—

"Come out! come out! I can't come in for I am dancing!"

The executioner said, "You can't know who I am! I chop the bad people's heads off, and I see that my ax is quivering."

"Don't chop my head off," said Karen, "for then I can never repent of my sins, but pray, pray chop off my feet with the red shoes!"

Then she confessed all her sins, and the

executioner chopped off her feet with the red shoes, and they danced away with the little feet into the depths of the forest.

Then he made her a pair of wooden feet and crutches, and he taught her the psalm, that penitents sing; and she kissed the hand which had wielded the ax, and went away over the heath.

"I have suffered enough for those red shoes!" said she. "I will go to church now, so that they may see me!" and she went as fast as she could to the church door. When she got there, the red shoes danced right up in front of her. She was so frightened that she went home again.

She was very sad all the week, and shed many bitter tears, but when Sunday came, she said, "Now then, I have suffered and struggled long enough; I should think I am quite as good as many who sit holding their heads so high in church!" She went along quite boldly, but she did not get further than the gate before she saw the red shoes dancing in front of her; she was more frightened than ever, and turned back, this time with real repentance in her heart. Then she went to the parson's house, and begged to be taken into service, she would be very industrious and work as hard as she could, she didn't care what wages they gave her, if only she might have a roof over her head and live among kind people. The parson's wife was sorry for her, and took her into her service. Karen became very industrious and thoughtful. She would sit and listen most attentively in the evening when the parson read the Bible. All the little ones were very fond of her, but when they chattered about finery and dress, and about being as beautiful as a queen, she would shake her head.

On Sunday they all went to church. When they asked her if she would go with them she looked sadly, with tears in her eyes, at her crutches, and they went without her to hear the word of God, while she sat in her little room alone. It was only big enough for a bed and a chair; she sat there with her prayer-book in her hand, and as she read it with a humble mind, she heard the notes of the organ, borne from the church by the wind, and she raised her tear-stained face and said, "Oh, God help me!"

Then the sun shone brightly round her, and the angel in the white robes whom she had seen on yonder night, at the church door, stood before her. He no longer held the sharp sword in his hand, but a beautiful green branch, covered with roses. He touched the ceiling with it and it rose to a great height, and wherever he touched it a golden star appeared. Then he touched the walls and they spread themselves out, and she saw and heard the organ. She saw the pictures of the old parsons and their wives; the congregation were all sitting in their seats singing aloud—for the church itself had come home to the poor girl, in her narrow little chamber, or else she had been taken to it. She found herself on the bench with the other people from the Parsonage. And when the hymn had come to an end they looked up and said, "It was fine that you came after all, little Karen!"

"It was through God's mercy!" she said. The organ sounded, and the children's voices echoed sweetly through the choir. The warm sunshine streamed brightly in through the window, right up to the bench where Karen sat; her heart was so overfilled with the sunshine, with peace, and with joy, that it broke. Her soul flew with the sunshine to heaven, and no one there ever asked about the red shoes.

The Steadfast Tin Soldier

THERE WERE ONCE five and twenty tin soldiers, all brothers, for they were the offspring of the same old tin spoon. Each man shouldered his gun, kept his eyes well to the front, and wore the smartest red and blue uniform imaginable. The first thing they heard in their new world, when the lid was taken off the box, was a little boy clapping his hands and crying, "Soldiers, soldiers!" It was his birthday and they had just been given to him; so he lost no time in setting them up on the table. All the soldiers were exactly alike with one exception, and he differed from the rest in having only one leg. For he was made last, and there was not quite enough tin left to finish him. However, he stood just as well on his one leg, as the others on two, in fact he is the very one who is to become famous. On the table where they were being set up, were many other toys; but the chief thing which

41

caught the eye was a delightful paper castle.
You could see through the tiny windows, right
into the rooms. Outside there were some little
trees surrounding a small mirror, representing
a lake, whose surface reflected the waxen
swans which were swimming about on it. It
was altogether charming, but the prettiest
thing of all was a little maiden standing at the
open door of the castle. She, too, was cut out
of paper, but she wore a dress of the lightest
gauze, with a dainty little blue ribbon over her
shoulders, by way of a scarf, set off by a bril-
liant spangle, as big as her whole face. The little maid was stretching out both arms, for she
was a dancer, and in the dance, one of her
legs was raised so high into the air that the tin
soldier could see absolutely nothing of it, and
supposed that she, like himself, had but one
leg.

"That would be the very wife for me!" he
thought; "but she is much too grand; she lives
in a palace, while I only have a box, and then
there are five and twenty of us to share it. No,
that would be no place for her, but I must try
to make her acquaintance!" Then he lay down
full length behind a snuff box, which stood on
the table. From that point he could have a
good look at the little lady, who continued to
stand on one leg without losing her balance.

But the prettiest thing of all was a little maiden
standing at the open door of the castle.

Late in the evening the other soldiers were put into their box, and the people of the house went to bed. Now was the time for the toys to play; they amused themselves with paying visits, fighting battles, and giving balls. The tin soldiers rustled about in their box, for they wanted to join the games, but they could not get the lid off. The nutcrackers turned somersaults, and the pencil scribbled nonsense on the slate. There was such a noise that the canary woke up and joined in, but his remarks were in verse. The only two who did not move were the tin soldier and the little dancer. She stood as stiff as ever on tiptoe, with her arms spread out; he was equally firm on his one leg, and he did not take his eyes off her for a moment.

Then the clock struck twelve, and pop! up flew the lid of the snuff box, but there was no snuff in it, no! There was a little black goblin, a sort of Jack-in-the-box.

"Tin soldier!" said the goblin, "have the goodness to keep your eyes to yourself."

But the tin soldier feigned not to hear.

"Ah! you just wait till to-morrow," said the goblin.

In the morning, when the children got up, they put the tin soldier on the window frame, and, whether it was caused by the goblin or by a puff of wind, I do not know, but all at once the window burst open, and the soldier fell head foremost from the third story.

It was a terrific descent, and he landed at last, with his leg in the air, and rested on his cap, with his bayonet fixed between two paving stones. The maid-servant and the little boy ran down at once to look for him, but although they almost trod on him, they could not see him. Had the soldier only called out, "Here I am," they would easily have found him, but he did not think it proper to shout when he was in uniform.

Presently it began to rain, and the drops fell faster and faster, till there was a regular torrent. When it was over two street boys came along.

"Look out!" said one; "there is a tin soldier! He shall go for a sail!"

So they made a boat out of a newspaper and put the soldier into the middle of it, and he sailed away down the gutter; both boys ran alongside clapping their hands. Good heavens! what waves there were in the gutter, and what a current, but then it certainly had rained cats and dogs. The paper boat danced up and down, and now and then whirled round and round. A shudder ran through the tin soldier, but he remained undaunted, and did not move a muscle, only looked straight before him with his gun shouldered. All at once the boat drifted under a long wooden tunnel, and it became as dark as it was in his box.

"Where am I going now!" thought he. "Well, well, it is all the fault of that goblin! Oh, if only the little maiden were with me in the boat it might be twice as dark for all I should care!"

At this moment a big water rat, who lived in the tunnel, came up.

"Have you a pass?" asked the rat. "Hand up your pass!"

The tin soldier did not speak, but clung still tighter to his gun. The boat rushed on, the rat close behind. Phew, how he gnashed his teeth and shouted to the bits of stick and straw.

"Stop him, stop him, he hasn't paid his toll! He hasn't shown his pass!"

But the current grew stronger and stronger, the tin soldier could already see daylight before him at the end of the tunnel; but he also heard a roaring sound, fit to strike terror to the bravest heart. Just imagine! Where the tunnel ended the stream rushed straight into the big canal. That would be just as dangerous for him as it would be for us to shoot a great rapid.

He was so near the end now that it was impossible to stop. The boat dashed out; the poor tin soldier held himself as stiff as he could; no one should say of him that he even winced.

The boat swirled round three or four times, and filled with water to the edge; it must sink. The tin soldier stood up to his neck in water, and the boat sank deeper and deeper. The paper became limper and limper, and at last the water went over his head—then he thought of the pretty little dancer, whom he was never to see again, and this refrain rang in his ears:

"Onward! Onward! Soldier!
For death thou canst not shun."

At last the paper gave way entirely and the soldier fell through—but at that moment he was swallowed by a big fish.

Oh! how dark it was inside the fish, it was worse than being in the tunnel even, and it was so narrow! But the tin soldier was as dauntless as ever, and lay full length shouldering his gun.

The fish rushed about and made the most frantic movements. At last it became quite quiet, and after a time, a flash like lightning pierced it. The soldier was once more in the broad daylight, and someone called out loudly, "A tin soldier!" The fish had been caught, taken to market, sold, and brought into the kitchen, where the cook cut it open with a large knife. She took the soldier up by the waist, with two fingers, and carried him into the parlor, where everyone wanted to see the wonderful man, who had traveled about in the stomach of a fish; but the tin soldier was not at all proud. They set him up on the table, and, wonder of wonders! he found himself in the very same room that he had been in before. He saw the very same children, and the toys were still standing on the table, as well as the beautiful castle with the pretty little dancer.

She still stood on one leg, and held the other up in the air. You see she also was unbending. The soldier was so much moved that he was ready to shed tears of tin, but that would not have been fitting. He looked at her, and she looked at him, but they said never a word. At this moment one of the little boys took up the tin soldier, and without rhyme or reason, threw him into the fire. No doubt the little goblin in the snuff box was to blame for that. The tin soldier stood there, lighted up by the flame, and in the most horrible heat; but whether it was the heat of the real fire, or the warmth of his feelings, he did not know. He had lost all his gay color; it might have been from his perilous journey, or it might have been from grief, who can tell?

He looked at the little maiden, and she looked at him, and he felt that he was melting away, but he still managed to keep himself erect, shouldering his gun bravely.

A door was suddenly opened, the draught caught the little dancer and she fluttered like a sylph, straight into the fire, to the soldier. When the maid took away the ashes next morning she found in them a small tin heart. But of the dancer nothing remained but the spangle, and that was burned as black as a coal.

Thumbelina

THERE WAS ONCE a woman who wished very much to have a little child, and at last she went to a fairy, and said, "I should so very much like to have a little child; can you tell me where I can find one?"

"Oh, that can be easily managed," said the fairy. "Here is a grain of barley different from the kind that grows in the fields and feeds the chickens; plant it in a flower pot and see what will happen."

"Thank you," said the woman, and she gave the fairy twelve pennies, then she went home and planted the barley corn, and immediately there grew up a large handsome flower, something like a tulip, but with its leaves tightly closed as if it were still a bud. "It is a beautiful flower," said the woman, and she kissed the red and golden-colored leaves. While she kissed the flower it opened, and she could see that it was a real tulip. Within the flower, upon the green velvet stamens, sat a very delicate and graceful little maiden. She was scarcely half as long as a thumb, so she was named "Thumbelina," because she was so small. A walnut-shell, elegantly polished, served her for a cradle; her mattress was made of blue violet-leaves, with a rose-leaf for a counter-pane. Here she slept at night, but during the day she amused herself on a table, where the woman had placed a plate full of water. Round this plate were flowers with their stems in the water, and upon it floated a large tulip-petal, which served Thumbelina for a boat. Here the little girl sat and rowed herself from side to side, with two oars made of white horsehair. It really was a very pretty sight. Thumbelina could sing so softly and sweetly that nothing so sweet had ever before been heard.

One night, while she lay in her pretty bed, a large, ugly, wet toad crept through a broken pane of glass in the window, and leaped right upon the table where Thumbelina lay sleeping under her rose-leaf quilt. "What a pretty little wife this would make for my son!" said the toad, and she took up the walnut-shell in which little Thumbelina lay asleep, and jumped through the window with it into the garden.

During the day she amused herself on a table, where the woman had placed a plate full of water.

In the swampy margin of a broad stream in the garden lived the toad, with her son. He was uglier even than his mother, and when he saw the pretty little maiden in her elegant bed, he could only cry, "Coax, Coax, Buk-ke-kex."

"Don't speak so loud, or she will awake," said the toad, "and then she might run away, for she is as light as swan's down. We will place her on one of the water-lily leaves out in the stream; it will be like an island to her, she is so light and small, and then she cannot escape; and, while she is away, we will make haste and prepare the state-room under the marsh, in which you are to live when you are married."

Far out in the stream grew a number of water-lilies, with broad green leaves, which seemed to float on the top of the water. The largest of these leaves appeared farther off than the rest, and the old toad swam out to it with the walnut-shell, in which little Thumbelina lay still asleep.

The little girl woke very early in the morning, and began to cry bitterly when she found where she was, for she could see nothing but water on every side of the large green leaf, and no way of reaching the land. Meanwhile the old toad was very busy under the marsh, decking her room with rushes and yellow wild flowers, to make it look pretty for her new daughter-in-law. Then she swam out with her ugly son to the leaf on which she had placed poor little Thumbelina. She wanted to fetch the pretty bed, to put it in the bridal chamber for her.

The old toad bowed low to her in the water, and said, "Here is my son; he will be your husband, and you will live happily together in the marsh by the stream."

"Coax, Coax, Buk-ke-kex," was all her son could say for himself; so the toad took up the elegant little bed, and swam away with it, leaving Thumbelina all alone on the green leaf, where she sat and wept. She could not bear to think of living with the old toad, and having her ugly son for a husband. The little fishes, who swam about in the water beneath, had seen the toad, and had heard what she said, so they lifted their heads above the water to look at the little maiden. They saw that she was very pretty, and it made them sorry to think that she must go and live with the ugly toads. "No, we must not allow that!" So they assembled in the water, round the green stalk which held the leaf on which the little maiden stood, and gnawed it away at the root with their teeth. Then the leaf floated down the stream, carrying Thumbelina far away, out of reach of land.

Thumbelina sailed past many towns, and the little birds in the bushes saw her, and sang, "What a lovely little creature!" so the leaf swam away with her farther and farther, till it brought her to other lands. A graceful white butterfly constantly fluttered round her, and at last alighted on the leaf. Thumbelina pleased him, and she was glad of it, for now the toad could not possibly reach her, and the country through which she sailed was beautiful, and the sun shone upon the water, till it glittered like liquid gold. She took off her girdle and tied one end of it round the butterfly, and the other end of the ribbon she fastened to the leaf, which now glided on much faster than ever, taking little Thumbelina with it as she stood. Presently a large June-bug flew by; the moment he caught sight of her, he seized her round her delicate waist with his claws, and flew with her into a tree. The green leaf floated away on the brook, and the butterfly flew with it, for he was fastened to it, and could not get away.

Oh, how frightened little Thumbelina felt when the June-bug flew with her to the tree! The beautiful white butterfly floated away with the leaf, but the June-bug did not trouble himself at all about that. He seated himself by her side on a large green leaf, gave her some honey from the flowers to eat, and told her she was very pretty, though not in the least like a June-bug. After a time, all the June-bugs who lived in the tree came to visit her. They stared at Thumbelina, and then the young lady June-bugs turned up their feelers, and said, "She has only two legs! how ugly that looks." "She has no feelers," said another. "Her waist is quite slim. Pooh! she is like a human being."

"Oh! she is ugly," said all the lady June-bugs, although Thumbelina was very pretty. Then the June-bug who had run away with her believed all the others when they said she was ugly, and would have nothing more to say to her, and told her she might go where she liked. He flew down with her from the tree, and placed her on a daisy, where she cried because she was so ugly that even the June-bugs would have nothing to do with her. And yet she was really the loveliest creature that one could imagine, and as tender and delicate as a beautiful rose-leaf. Poor little Thumbelina lived quite alone in the wide forest all that summer. She wove herself a bed with blades of grass, and hung it up under a broad leaf, to protect herself from the rain. She sucked the

honey from the flowers for food, and drank
the dew from their leaves every morning. So
the summer and the autumn passed away, and
then came the winter—the long, cold winter.
All the birds who had sung to her so sweetly
flew away, and the trees and the flowers were
withered. The large clover leaf, under which
she had lived, had shriveled up, and left nothing but a dry yellow stalk. She shivered with
cold, for her clothes were worn out. It began
to snow and each flake was like a whole shov-
elful falling upon one of us, for we are large,
but she was only an inch high. Then she
wrapped herself up in a dry leaf, but that
cracked in the middle, and did not keep her
warm, and she shook with cold.

Near the wood in which she had been living
lay a large corn-field, but the corn had been
cut a long time, and nothing remained but the
bare, dry stubble standing up out of the frozen ground. It was like a large wood to her.
Oh! how she shivered with the cold. She came
at last to the door of a field-mouse, who had a
little home under the corn-stubble. The field-
mouse lived there, warm and comfortable,
with a whole roomful of corn, a kitchen, and a
beautiful dining-room. Poor little Thumbelina
stood before the door like a little beggar-girl,

and begged for a small piece of barleycorn, for she had been without a morsel to eat for two long days.

"You poor little creature," said the field-mouse, who was really a good old field-mouse, "come into my warm room and dine with me." She was so pleased with Thumbelina that she said, "You are quite welcome to stay with me all the winter, if you like; but you must keep my rooms clean and neat, and tell me stories, for I like them very much." So Thumbelina did all the field-mouse desired, and was very comfortable on the whole.

One day the field-mouse said, "We shall have a visitor soon. My neighbor pays me a visit once a week. He is better off than I am; he has large rooms, and wears a beautiful black velvet coat. If you could only have him for a husband, you would be well provided for indeed. But he is blind, so you must tell him the prettiest stories you know."

But Thumbelina did not feel at all interested in this neighbor, for he was a mole. However, he came and paid his visit, dressed in his black velvet coat.

"He is very rich and learned, and his house is twenty times larger than mine," said the field-mouse.

He was rich and learned, no doubt, but he
always spoke slightingly of the sun and the
pretty flowers, because he had never seen
them. Thumbelina was obliged to sing to him,
"Lady-bird, lady-bird, fly away home," and
many other pretty songs. And the mole fell in
love with her sweet voice. A short time
before, he had dug a long passage under the
earth, which led from the dwelling of the
field-mouse to his own, and the field-mouse
and Thumbelina had permission to walk
whenever they liked. He warned them not to
be afraid of a dead bird that lay in the passage. The mole took a piece of phosphorescent wood in his mouth; it shone like fire in
the dark and he led them through the long,
dark passage. When they came to the spot
where the dead bird lay, the mole pushed his
broad nose through the ceiling, so as to make
a large hole, through which the daylight shone
into the passage. In the middle of the floor lay
a dead swallow, his beautiful wings folded
close to his sides, his feet and his head drawn
up under his feathers. It made little Thumbelina very sad to see it, she so loved the little
birds who had sung and twittered for her so
beautifully all summer. But the mole pushed it
aside with his crooked legs, and said, "He will

sing no more now. How miserable it must be to be born a little bird! I am thankful that none of my children will ever be birds."

"Yes," exclaimed the field-mouse. "What is the use of his twittering, for when winter comes he must either starve or be frozen to death. Still, birds are very high bred."

Thumbelina said nothing; but when the two others had turned their backs on the bird, she stooped down and stroked the soft feathers of his head, and kissed the closed eyelids. "Perhaps this was the very one who sang to me so sweetly in the summer," she said; "and how much pleasure you gave me, you dear, pretty bird."

The mole now stopped up the hole through which the daylight shone, and led the ladies home again. But during the night Thumbelina could not sleep, so she got out of bed and wove a large, beautiful rug of hay. She carried it to the dead bird, and spread it over him, with some down from the flowers which she had found in the field-mouse's room. It was as soft as wool, and she spread some of it on each side of the bird, so that he might lie warmly in the cold earth.

"Farewell, pretty bird," said she, "farewell and thank you for your sweet singing through the summer, when all the trees were green, and the warm sun shone upon us." Then she laid her head on the bird's breast, but she was startled, for it seemed as if something inside the bird went "thump, thump." It was the bird's heart. He was not really dead, only numbed with the cold, and the warmth was restoring him to life.

In autumn, all the swallows fly away to warm countries, but if one happens to linger, the cold seizes it, it falls and remains where it fell, until the cold snow covers it. Thumbelina trembled; she was quite frightened, for the bird was large, a great deal larger than herself—she was only an inch high. But she took courage, laid the wool more thickly over the poor swallow, and then brought a leaf which she had used for her own counterpane, and laid it over the head of the poor bird.

The next night she again stole out to see him. He was alive but very weak; he could only open his eyes for a moment to look at Thumbelina, who stood holding a piece of phosphorescent wood in her hand, for she had no other lantern.

"Thank you, pretty child," said the sick swallow; "I have been so nicely warmed, that I shall be strong again and able to fly about in the warm sunshine."

"Oh," said she, "it is cold outdoors now; it

snows and freezes. Stay in your warm bed! I will take care of you!"

She brought the swallow some water in a flower-leaf, and, after he had drunk, he told her that he had wounded one of his wings in a thorn-bush, and could not fly as fast as the others, who were soon far away on their journey to warm countries. At last he had fallen and could remember no more, nor how he came where she had found him. The whole winter the swallow remained underground, and Thumbelina nursed him with care and love. Neither the mole nor the field-mouse knew anything about it, for they did not like swallows.

The spring came, and the sun warmed the earth. Then the swallow bade farewell to Thumbelina, and she opened the hole which the mole had made in the ceiling. The sun shone in upon them so beautifully, that the swallow asked her if she would go with him; she could sit on his back, he said, and he would fly away with her into the green woods. But Thumbelina knew it would make the field-mouse sad if she left her that way, so she said, "No, I cannot."

"Farewell, then, farewell, you good, pretty little girl," said the swallow and flew out into the sunshine.

Thumbelina looked after him, and the tears rose in her eyes for she was very fond of the swallow.

"Tweet, tweet," sang the bird, flying out into the green woods. Thumbelina felt very sad. She was not allowed to go out into the warm sunshine. The corn which had been sown in the field over the house of the field-mouse had grown high into the air; it was a thick wood to Thumbelina, who was only an inch high.

"You are going to be married, Thumbelina," said the field-mouse. "My neighbor has asked for you. What good fortune for a poor child like you! Now we will make your wedding clothes. They must be both woolen and linen. Nothing must be wanting when you are the mole's wife."

Thumbelina had to turn the spinning wheel, and the field-mouse hired four spiders, who were to weave day and night. Every evening the mole visited her, and was always speaking of the time when the summer would be over. Then he would keep his wedding-day with Thumbelina; but now the heat of the sun was so great that it burned the earth, and made it quite hard, like a stone. As soon as the summer was over, the wedding should take place.

But Thumbelina was not happy; for she did not like the tiresome mole. Every morning when the sun rose, and every evening when it went down, she would creep out at the door, and as the wind blew aside the leaves of the corn, so that she could see the blue sky, she thought how beautiful and bright it seemed out there, and wished so much to see her dear swallow again.

When autumn arrived, Thumbelina's outfit was ready, and the field-mouse said, "In four weeks the wedding must take place."

Then Thumbelina cried, and said she did not want to marry the tiresome mole.

"Nonsense," replied the field-mouse. "Don't be foolish. He is a very handsome mole; the queen herself does not wear more beautiful velvets and furs. His kitchens and cellars are quite full. You ought to be thankful for such good fortune."

So the wedding-day was fixed, and the mole was to take Thumbelina to live with him, deep under the earth, and never again to see the warm sun, because he did not like it. The field-mouse had given her permission to stand at the door before she left.

"Farewell, bright sun," she cried, stretching out her arm towards it and she walked a short distance from the house, for the corn had been cut and only the dry stubble was left in the fields. "Farewell, farewell," she repeated, twining her arm round a little red flower. "Greet the little swallow from me, if you should see him again."

"Tweet, tweet," sounded over her head. She looked up, and there was the swallow himself flying close by. As soon as he spied Thumbelina, he was delighted. She told him how she was to marry the ugly mole, and how unhappy she felt that she must live always beneath the earth, and never see the bright sun any more. And as she told him, she wept.

"Cold winter is coming," said the swallow, "and I am going to fly away into warmer countries. Will you go with me? You can sit on my back, and fasten yourself on with your sash. Then we can fly away from the ugly mole and his gloomy home—far away, over the mountains, to warm countries, where the sun shines more brightly than here; where it is always summer, and the flowers are always in bloom. Fly now with me, dear little Thumbelina—you who saved my life when I lay frozen in that dark, dreary passage."

"Yes, I will go with you," said Thumbelina. She seated herself on the bird's back, with her feet on his outstretched wings, and tied her girdle to one of his strongest feathers.

Then the swallow rose in the air, and flew over forest and over sea, high above the highest mountains, covered with snow that never melts. Thumbelina would have been frozen in the cold air, but she crept under the bird's warm feathers, keeping her little head uncovered, so that she might admire the beautiful lands over which they passed. At length they reached the warm countries, where the sun shines more brightly, and the sky seems much higher above the earth. Here, on the hedges, and by the wayside, grew purple, green, and white grapes, and lemons and oranges hung from trees in the woods; the air was fragrant with myrtles and orange blossoms. Beautiful children ran along the country lanes, playing with gay butterflies; and as the swallow flew farther and farther, every place appeared still more lovely.

At last they came to a blue lake, and by the side of it, shaded by trees of the deepest green, stood a palace of dazzling white marble, built in ancient times. Vines clustered round its lofty pillars, and at the top were many swallows' nests; one of these was the home of the swallow who carried Thumbelina.

"This is my house," said the swallow; "but you would not be comfortable in it. Choose one of those lovely flowers, and I will put you down upon it, and then you shall have everything that you can wish to make you happy."

"That will be delightful," said Thumbelina, clapping her little hands.

A marble pillar had fallen to the ground, and lay there broken into three pieces. Between these pieces grew most beautiful large white flowers. The swallow flew down with Thumbelina, and placed her on one of the broad leaves. How astonished she was to see, in the middle of the flower, a tiny little man, as white and transparent as if he had been made of crystal! He had a gold crown on his head, and delicate wings at his shoulders, and was not much larger than Thumbelina herself. He was the angel of the flower; for a tiny man or a tiny woman dwells in every flower; and this was the king of them all.

"Oh, how beautiful he is!" whispered Thumbelina to the swallow.

The little prince was at first quite frightened at the bird, who was like a giant, compared to such a delicate little creature as himself; but when he saw Thumbelina, he was delighted. She was the prettiest little maid he had ever seen. He took the gold crown from his head, and placed it on hers, and asked her name, and if she would be his queen of all the flowers.

So she said, "Yes," to the handsome prince. Then all the flowers opened, and out of each came a little lady or a tiny lord, all so pretty that it was a pleasure to look at them. Each of them brought Thumbelina a present. The best gift was a pair of beautiful wings, which had belonged to a large white fly. They were fastened to Thumbelina's shoulders, so that she might fly from flower to flower. Then there was much rejoicing, and the little swallow, who sat above them, in his nest, was asked to sing a wedding song, which he did as well as he could; but in his heart he felt sad, for he was very fond of Thumbelina, and would have liked never to part from her again.

"You must not be called Thumbelina any more," said the spirit of the flowers to her. "It is an ugly name, and you are so very pretty. We will call you May."

"Farewell, farewell," said the swallow, as he left the warm countries, to fly back into Denmark. There he had a nest over the window of a house in which dwelt the man who wrote this story. The swallow sang, "Tweet, tweet," and from his song came the whole story.

The Little Match Girl

IT WAS TERRIBLY COLD; it snowed and
was already almost dark, and evening came
on, the last evening of the year. In the cold
and gloom a poor little girl, bare headed and
barefoot, was walking through the streets.
When she left her own house she certainly
had had slippers on; but of what use were
they? They were very big slippers, and her
mother had used them till then, so big were
they. The little maid lost them as she slipped
across the road, where two carriages were
rattling by terribly fast. One slipper was not to
be found again, and a boy had seized the
other, and run away with it. He thought he
could use it very well as a cradle, some day
when he had children of his own. So now the
little girl went with her little naked feet,
which were quite red and blue with the cold.
In an old apron she carried a number of
matches, and a bundle of them in her hand.

No one had bought anything of her all day, and no one had given her a farthing.

Shivering with cold and hunger she crept along, a picture of misery, poor little girl! The snowflakes covered her long fair hair, which fell in pretty curls over her neck; but she did not think of that now. In all the windows lights were shining, and there was a glorious smell of roast goose, for it was New Year's Eve. Yes, she thought of that!

In a corner formed by two houses, one of which projected beyond the other, she sat down, cowering. She had drawn up her little feet, but she was still colder, and she did not dare to go home, for she had sold no matches, and did not bring a farthing of money. From her father she would certainly receive a beating, and besides, it was cold at home, for they had nothing over them but a roof through which the wind whistled, though the largest rents had been stopped with straw and rags.

Her little hands were almost benumbed with the cold. Ah! a match might do her good, if she could only draw one from the bundle, and rub it against the wall, and warm her hands at it. She drew one out. R-r-atch! how it sputtered and burned! It was a warm bright flame, like a little candle, when she held her hands over it; it was a wonderful little light! It really seemed to the little girl as if she sat before a great polished stove, with bright brass feet and a brass cover. How the fire burned! how comfortable it was! but the little flame went out, the stove vanished, and she had only the remains of the burned match in her hand.

A second was rubbed against the wall. It burned up, and when the light fell upon the wall it became transparent like a thin veil, and she could see through it into the room. On the table a snow-white cloth was spread; upon it stood a shining dinner service; the roast goose smoked gloriously, stuffed with apples and dried plums. And what was still more splendid to behold, the goose hopped down from the dish, and waddled along the floor, with a knife and fork in its breast, to the little girl. Then the match went out, and only the thick, damp, cold wall was before her. She lighted another match. Then she was sitting under a beautiful Christmas tree; it was greater and more ornamented than the one she had seen through the glass door at the rich merchant's. Thousands of candles burned upon the green branches, and colored pictures like those in the print shops looked down upon them. The little girl stretched forth her hand towards them; then the match went out. The Christmas lights mounted higher. She saw them now as stars in the sky: one of them fell down, forming a long line of fire.

"Now some one is dying," thought the little girl, for her old grandmother, the only person who had loved her, and who was now dead, had told her that when a star fell down a soul mounted up to God.

She rubbed another match against the wall; it became bright again, and in the brightness the old grandmother stood clear and shining, mild and lovely.

"Grandmother!" cried the child, "Oh! take me with you! I know you will go when the match is burned out. You will vanish like the warm fire, the warm food, and the great glorious Christmas tree!"

And she hastily rubbed the whole bundle of matches, for she wished to hold her grandmother fast. And the matches burned with such a glow that it became brighter than in the middle of the day; grandmother had never been so large or so beautiful. She took the little girl in her arms, and both flew in brightness and joy above the earth, very, very high, and up there was neither cold, nor hunger, nor care—they were with God!

But in the corner, leaning against the wall,

sat the poor girl with red cheeks and smiling mouth, frozen to death on the last evening of the Old Year. The New Year's sun rose upon a little corpse! The child sat there, stiff and cold, with the matches of which one bundle was burned. "She wanted to warm herself," the people said. No one imagined what a beautiful thing she had seen, and in what glory she had gone in with her grandmother to the New Year's Day.

The Nightingale

IN CHINA, the emperor is a Chinaman, and
all the people around him are Chinamen,
too. It is many years since the story I am
going to tell you happened, but that is all the
more reason for telling it, lest it should be for-
gotten. The emperor's palace was the most
beautiful thing in the world; it was made
entirely of the finest porcelain, very costly,
but at the same time so fragile that it could
only be touched with the very greatest care.
There were the most extraordinary flowers to
be seen in the garden; the most beautiful ones
had little silver bells tied to them, which tin-
kled perpetually, so that one could not pass
the flowers without looking at them. Every little detail in the garden had been most carefully thought out, and it was so big, that even
the gardener himself did not know where it
ended. If one went on walking, one came to
beautiful woods with lofty trees and deep

lakes. The wood extended to the sea, which
was deep and blue, deep enough for large
ships to sail right up under the branches of
the trees. Among these trees lived a nightingale, which sang so deliciously, that even the
poor fisherman who had plenty of other things
to do, lay still to listen to it, when he was out
at night drawing in his nets. "Heavens, how
beautiful it is!" he said, but then he had to
attend to his business and forgot it. The next
night when he heard it again he would again
exclaim, "Heavens, how beautiful it is!"

Travelers came to the emperor's capital,
from every country in the world; they admired
everything very much, especially the palace
and the gardens, but when they heard the
nightingale they all said, "This is better than
anything!"

When they got home they described it, and
the learned ones wrote many books about the
town, the palace and the garden, but nobody
forgot the nightingale, it was always put
above everything else. Those among them
who were poets wrote the most beautiful
poems, all about the nightingale in the woods
by the deep blue sea. These books went all
over the world, and in course of time, some of
them reached the emperor. He sat in his
golden chair reading and reading, and nod-

ding his head, well pleased to hear such beautiful descriptions of the town, the palace and the garden. "But the nightingale is the best of all," he read.

"What is this?" said the emperor. "The nightingale? Why, I know nothing about it. Is there such a bird in my kingdom, and in my own garden into the bargain, and I have never heard of it? Imagine my having to discover this from a book!"

Then he called his gentleman-in-waiting, who was so grand that when anyone of a lower rank dared to speak to him, or to ask him a question, he would only answer "P," which means nothing at all.

"There is said to be a very wonderful bird called a nightingale here," said the emperor. "They say that it is better than anything else in all my great kingdom! Why have I never been told anything about it?"

"I have never heard it mentioned," said the gentleman-in-waiting. "It has never been presented at court."

"I wish it to appear here this evening to sing to me," said the emperor. "The whole world knows what I am possessed of, and I know nothing about it!"

"I have never heard it mentioned before," said the gentleman-in-waiting. "I will seek it, and I will find it!" But where was it to be found? The gentleman-in-waiting ran upstairs and downstairs and in and out of all the rooms and corridors. No one of all those he met had ever heard anything about the nightingale; so the gentleman-in-waiting ran back to the emperor, and said that it must be a myth, invented by the writers of the books. "Your imperial majesty must not believe everything that is written; books are often mere inventions, even if they do not belong to what we call the black art!"

"But this book was sent to me by the powerful Emperor of Japan, so it can't be untrue. I will hear this nightingale; I insist upon its being here to-night. I extend my most gracious protection to it, and if it is not forthcoming, I will have the whole court trampled upon after supper!"

"Tsing-pe!" said the gentleman-in-waiting, and away he ran again, up and down all the stairs, in and out of all the rooms and corridors; half the court ran with him, for they none of them wished to be trampled on. There was much questioning about this nightingale, which was known to all the outside world, but to no one at court. At last they found a poor little maid in the kitchen. She said, "Oh heavens, the nightingale? I know it very well. Yes, indeed it can sing. Every evening I am allowed to take broken meat to my poor sick mother:

she lives down by the shore. On my way back, when I am tired, I rest a while in the wood, and then I hear the nightingale. Its song brings the tears into my eyes, I feel as if my mother were kissing me!"

"Little kitchen maid," said the gentleman-in-waiting, "I will procure you a permanent position in the kitchen and permission to see the emperor dining, if you will take us to the nightingale. It is commanded to appear at court to-night."

Then they all went out into the wood where the nightingale usually sang. Half the court was there. As they were going along at their best pace a cow began to bellow.

"Oh!" said a young courtier, "there we have 'it. What wonderful power for such a little creature; I have certainly heard it before."

"No, those are the cows bellowing, we are a long way yet from the place."

Then the frogs began to croak in the marsh.

"Beautiful!" said the Chinese chaplain; "it is just like the tinkling of church bells."

"No, those are the frogs!" said the little kitchen maid. "But I think we shall soon hear it now!"

Then the nightingale began to sing.

"There it is!" said the little girl. "Listen, listen, there it sits!" and she pointed to a little gray bird up among the branches.

"Is it possible?" said the gentleman-in-waiting. "I should never have thought it was like that. How common it looks. Seeing so many grand people must have frightened all its colors away."

"Little nightingale!" called the kitchen maid quite loud, "our gracious emperor wishes to hear you sing to him!"

"With the greatest pleasure!" said the nightingale, warbling away in the most delightful fashion.

"It is just like crystal bells," said the gentleman-in-waiting. "Look at its little throat, how active it is. It is extraordinary that we have never heard of it before! I am sure it will be a great success at court!"

"Shall I sing again to the emperor?" said the nightingale, who thought he was present.

"My precious little nightingale," said the gentleman-in-waiting, "I have the honor to command your attendance at a court festival to-night, where you will charm his gracious majesty the emperor with your fascinating singing."

"It sounds best among the trees," said the nightingale, but it went with them willingly when it heard that the emperor wished it.

The palace had been brightened up for the occasion. The walls and the floors, which were all of china, shone by the light of many thousand golden lamps. The most beautiful flowers, all of the tinkling kind, were arranged in the corridors; there was hurrying to and fro, and one's ears were full of the tinkling. In the middle of the large reception room, where the emperor sat, a golden rod had been fixed, on which the nightingale was to perch. The whole court was assembled, and the little kitchen maid had been permitted to stand behind the door, as she now had the actual title of cook. They were all dressed in their best; everybody's eyes were turned towards the little gray bird at which the emperor was nodding. The nightingale sang delightfully, and the tears came into the emperor's eyes, nay, they rolled down his cheeks. The nightingale sang more beautifully than ever; its notes touched all hearts. The emperor was charmed, and said the nightingale should have his gold slipper to wear round its neck. But the nightingale declined with thanks, it had already been sufficiently rewarded.

"I have seen tears in the eyes of the emperor, that is my richest reward. The tears of an emperor have a wonderful power! God knows I am sufficiently recompensed!" and then it again burst into its sweet heavenly song.

"That is the most delightful coquetting I

have ever seen!" said the ladies, and they took some water into their mouths to try and make the same gurgling when anyone spoke to them, thinking so to equal the nightingale. Even the lackeys and the chambermaids announced that they were satisfied, and that is saying a great deal, they are always the most difficult people to please. Yes, indeed, the nightingale had made a sensation. It was to stay at court now, and to have its own cage, as well as liberty to walk out twice a day, and once in the night. It always had twelve foot-men, each one holding a ribbon which was tied round its leg. There was not much plea-sure in an outing of that sort.

The whole town talked about the marvelous bird, and if two people met, one said to the other "Night," and the other answered "Gale," and then they sighed, perfectly understanding each other. Eleven cheese-mongers' children were named for it, but they had not a voice among them.

One day a large parcel came for the emperor, outside was written the word "Nightingale."

"Here we have another new book about this celebrated bird," said the emperor. But it was no book, it was a little work of art in a box, an artificial nightingale, exactly like the liv-

ing one, but it was studded all over with diamonds, rubies, and sapphires.

When the bird was wound up, it could sing
one of the songs the real one sang, and it
wagged its tail which glittered with silver and
gold. A ribbon was tied round its neck on
which was written, "The Emperor of Japan's
nightingale is very poor, compared to the
Emperor of China's."

Everybody said, "Oh, how beautiful!" And
the person who brought the artificial bird
immediately received the title of Imperial
Nightingale-Carrier in Chief.

"Now, they must sing together. What a duet
that will be!"

Then they had to sing together, but they did
not get on very well, for the real nightingale
sang in its own way, and the artificial one
could only sing waltzes.

"There is no fault in that," said the music
master; "it is perfectly in time and correct in
every way!"

Then the artificial bird had to sing alone. It
was just as great a success as the real one,
besides it was so much prettier to look at; it
glittered like bracelets and breast-pins.

It sang the same tune three and thirty times
over, and yet it was not tired; people would
willingly have heard it from the beginning

again, but the emperor said that the real one must have a turn now—but where was it? No one had noticed that it had flown out of the open window, back to its own green woods.

"But what is the meaning of this?" said the emperor.

All the courtiers railed at it, and said it was a most ungrateful bird.

"We have got the best bird, though," said they, and then the artificial bird had to sing again, and this was the thirty-fourth time they heard the same tune, but they did not know it thoroughly even yet; it was so difficult.

The music master praised the bird tremendously, and insisted that it was much better than the real nightingale, not only as regarded the outside with all the diamonds, but the inside, too.

"Because you see, my ladies and gentlemen, and the emperor before all, in the real nightingale you never know what you will hear, but in the artificial one everything is decided beforehand! So it is, and so it must remain, it can't be otherwise. You can account for things, you can open it and show the human ingenuity in arranging the waltzes, how they go, and how one note follows upon another!"

"Those are exactly my opinions," they all said, and the music master got leave to show the bird to the public, next Sunday. They might also hear it sing, said the emperor. So they heard it, and all became as enthusiastic over it as if they had drunk themselves merry on tea—a thoroughly Chinese habit.

Then they all said, "Oh," and stuck their forefingers in the air and nodded their heads; but the poor fishermen who had heard the real nightingale said, "It sounds very nice, and it is very like the real one, but there is something wanting, we don't know what." The real nightingale was banished from the kingdom.

The artificial bird had its place on a silken cushion, close to the emperor's bed: all the presents it had received of gold and precious jewels were scattered round it. Its title had risen to be "Chief Imperial Singer of the Bed-Chamber," in rank number one, on the left side; for the emperor reckoned that side the important one, where the heart was seated. Even an emperor's heart is on the left side. The music master wrote five and twenty volumes about the artificial bird; the treatise was very long, and written in all the most difficult Chinese characters. Everybody said they had read and understood it, for otherwise they would have been reckoned stupid and then their bodies would have been trampled upon.

Things went on in this way for a whole year.

The emperor, the court, and all the other Chinamen knew every little gurgle in the song of the artificial bird by heart; but they liked it all the better for this, and they could all join in the song themselves. Even the street boys sang "zizizi" and "cluck, cluck, cluck," and the emperor sang it, too.

But, one evening, when the bird was singing its best, and the emperor was lying in bed listening to it, something gave way inside the bird with a "whizz." Then a spring burst; "whirr" went all the wheels and the music stopped. The emperor jumped out of bed and sent for his private physicians, but what good could they do? Then they sent for the watch-maker, and after a good deal of talk and examination, he got the works to go again, somehow; but he said it would have to be saved as much as possible, because it was so worn out, and he could not renew the works so as to be sure of the tune. This was a great blow! They only dared to let the artificial bird sing once a year, and hardly that; but then the music master made a little speech using all the most difficult words. He said it was just as good as ever, and his saying made it so.

Five years now passed, and then a great grief came upon the nation, for they were all very fond of their emperor. It was said he was ill and could not live. A new emperor was already chosen, and people stood about in the street, and asked the gentleman-in-waiting how their emperor was going on.

"P," answered he, shaking his head.

The emperor lay pale and cold in his gorgeous bed. The courtiers thought he was dead, and they all went off to pay their respects to their new emperor. The lackeys ran off to talk matters over, and the chambermaids gave a great coffee party. Cloth had been laid down in all the rooms and corridors so as to deaden the sound of footsteps, so it was very, very quiet. But the emperor was not dead yet. He lay stiff and pale in the gorgeous bed with its velvet hangings and heavy golden tassels. There was an open window high above him, and the moon streamed in upon the emperor, and the artificial bird beside him.

The poor emperor could hardly breathe; he seemed to have a weight on his chest. He opened his eyes and saw that it was Death sitting upon his chest, wearing his golden crown. In one hand he held the emperor's golden sword, and in the other his imperial banner. Round about, from among the folds of the velvet hangings peered many curious faces, some were hideous, others gentle and pleasant. They were all the emperor's good and bad deeds, which now looked him in the face when Death was weighing him down.

"Do you remember that?" whispered one after the other. "Do you remember this?" and they told him so many things, that the perspiration poured down his face.

"I never knew that," said the emperor. "Music, music, sound the great Chinese drums!" he cried, "that I may not hear what they are saying." But they went on and on, and Death sat nodding his head, just like a Chinaman, at everything that was said.

"Music, music!" shrieked the emperor. "You precious little golden bird, sing, sing! I have loaded you with precious stones, and even hung my own golden slipper round your neck. Sing, I tell you, sing!"

But the bird stood silent, there was nobody to wind it up, so of course it could not go. Death continued to fix the great empty sockets of its eyes upon the emperor, and all was silent, so terribly silent.

Suddenly, close to the window, there was a burst of lovely song; it was the living nightingale, perched on a branch outside. It had heard of the emperor's need, and had come to bring comfort and hope to him. And as it sang, the faces round the emperor became fainter and fainter, and the blood coursed with fresh vigor in his veins and through his feeble limbs. Even Death himself listened to the song and said, "Go on, little nightingale, go on!"

"Yes, if you give me the gorgeous golden sword; yes, if you give me the imperial banner; yes, if you give me the emperor's crown."

And Death gave back each of these treasures for a song, and the nightingale went on singing. It sang about the quiet churchyard, where the roses bloom, where the elder flower scents the air, and where the fresh grass is ever moistened anew by the tears of the mourner. This song brought to Death a longing for his own garden, and like a cold gray mist, he passed out of the window.

"Thanks, thanks!" said the emperor; "you heavenly little bird, I know you! I banished you from my kingdom, and yet you have charmed the evil visions away from my bed by your song, and even Death away from my heart! How can I ever repay you?"

"You have rewarded me," said the nightingale. "I brought the tears to your eyes, the very first time I ever sang to you, and I shall never forget it! Those are the jewels which gladden the heart of a singer. But sleep now, and wake up fresh and strong! I will sing to you!"

Then it sang again, and the emperor fell
into a sweet refreshing sleep. The sun shone
in at his window, when he woke fresh and
well; none of his attendants had yet come
back to him, for they thought he was dead,
but the nightingale still sat there singing.

"You must always stay with me!" said the
emperor. "You shall only sing when you like,
and I will break the artificial bird into a thousand pieces!"

"Don't do that!" said the nightingale, "it did
all the good it could! Keep it as you have
always done! I can't build my nest and live in
this palace, but let me come whenever I like,
then I will sit on the branch in the evening
and sing to you. I will sing to cheer you and to
make you thoughtful, too; I will sing to you of
the happy ones, and of those that suffer; I will
sing about the good and the evil, which are
kept hidden from you. The little singing bird
flies far and wide, to the poor fisherman and
the peasant's home, to numbers who are far
from you and your court. I love your heart
more than your crown, and yet there is an
odor of sanctity round the crown, too!—I will
come, and I will sing to you!—But you must
promise me one thing!"—

"Everything!" said the emperor, who stood
there in his imperial robes which he had just

Then it sang again, and the emperor fell into a
sweet refreshing sleep.

put on, and he held the sword heavy with gold upon his heart.

"One thing I ask you! Tell no one that you have a little bird who tells you everything. It will be better so!"

Then the nightingale flew away. The attendants came in to see their dead emperor, and there he stood, bidding them "Good-morning!"